鲁拜集

THE RUBAIYAT

[波斯]奥玛珈音 著
[英国]爱德华·菲茨杰拉德 英译
[美国]黄克孙 汉译

译林出版社

图书在版编目（CIP）数据

鲁拜集 /（波斯）奥玛珈音著；（英）菲茨杰拉德(Edward FitzGerald) 英译；(美) 黄克孙汉译 .—南京：译林出版社，2020.11 (2023.4 重印)
ISBN 978-7-5447-8375-0

Ⅰ. ①鲁…　Ⅱ. ①奥…②菲…③黄…　Ⅲ. ①诗集－伊朗－中世纪　Ⅳ. ①I373.23

中国版本图书馆 CIP 数据核字（2020）第153325号

著作权合同登记号　图字：10-2018-359号

鲁拜集　[波斯] 奥玛珈音 / 著　[英国] 爱德华 · 菲茨杰拉德 / 英译
[美国] 黄克孙 / 汉译

责任编辑　王　维
插　　图　埃德蒙 · 杜赖克　罗伯特 · 斯图尔特 · 谢里夫斯
装帧设计　韦　枫
校　　对　蒋　艳
责任印制　董　虎

出版发行　译林出版社
地　　址　南京市湖南路 1 号 A 楼
邮　　箱　yilin@yilin.com
网　　址　www.yilin.com
市场热线　025-86633278
排　　版　南京展望文化发展有限公司
印　　刷　南京爱德印刷有限公司
开　　本　890 毫米 ×1240 毫米　1/32
印　　张　6.875
插　　页　36
版　　次　2020 年 11 月第 1 版
印　　次　2023 年 4 月第 4 次印刷
书　　号　ISBN 978-7-5447-8375-0
定　　价　65.00 元

奥玛珈音

Omar Khayyam
（1048—1131）

波斯数学家、天文学家、哲学家、诗人，在三次方程式和历法领域成就杰出，创作了一千多首“鲁拜”，即波斯的四行诗，19 世纪英国诗人爱德华·菲茨杰拉德将其中百余首译为英语，结集为《鲁拜集》。

爱德华·菲茨杰拉德

Edward FitzGerald

（1809—1883）

又译费氏结楼，英国作家、诗人，毕业于剑桥大学三一学院，由于家族富有，一生过着隐居的乡绅生活，以翻译《鲁拜集》而闻名于世。

黄克孙

Kerson Huang

（1928—2016）

1928 年生于广西南宁。于 1953 年获得美国麻省理工学院物理博士学位。物理著作除学术论文外，有《统计力学》及《量子场论》等英文专著多种。人文方面著作有《易经》英译本、《鲁拜集》中译本，及诗集《沧江集》。

埃德蒙·杜赖克

Edmund Dulac
（1882—1953）

画家、设计师，生于法国，定居英国，为杂志、书籍绘制了大量插画，设计过邮票。他为图书绘制的插画多以礼品书形式出版，代表作品包括《一千零一夜》《安徒生童话》《睡美人和其他童话故事》《鲁拜集》等。

I. WAKE! For the Sun, who scatter'd into flight
The Stars before him from the Field of Night,
Drives Night along with them from Heav'n, and strikes
The Sultan's Turret with a Shaft of Light.

XI. With me along the strip of Herbage strown
That just divides the desert from the sown,
Where name of Slave and Sultan is forgot—
And Peace to Mahmúd on his golden Throne!

XII. A Book of Verses underneath the Bough,
A Jug of Wine, a Loaf of Bread—and Thou
Beside me singing in the Wilderness—
Oh, Wilderness were Paradise enow!

XIV. Look to the blowing Rose about us—"Lo,
Laughing," she says, "into the world I blow,
At once the silken tassel of my Purse
Tear, and its Treasure on the Garden throw."

XXII. For some we loved, the loveliest and the best
That from his Vintage rolling Time hath prest,
  Have drunk their Cup a Round or two before,
And one by one crept silently to rest.

XXXVII. For I remember stopping by the way
To watch a Potter thumping his wet Clay:
    And with its all-obliterated Tongue
It murmur'd—"Gently, Brother, gently, pray!"

XLI. Perplext no more with Human or Divine,
To-morrow's tangle to the winds resign,
    And lose your fingers in the tresses of
The Cypress-slender Minister of Wine.

XLV. 'Tis but a Tent where takes his one day's rest
A Sultan to the realm of Death addrest;
The Sultan rises, and the dark Ferrash
Strikes, and prepares it for another Guest.

LV. You know, my Friends, with what a brave Carouse
I made a Second Marriage in my house;
Divorced old barren Reason from my Bed,
And took the Daughter of the Vine to Spouse.

LVIII. And lately, by the Tavern Door agape,
Came shining through the Dusk an Angel Shape
  Bearing a Vessel on his Shoulder; and
He bid me taste of it; and 'twas—the Grape!

LXV. The Revelations of Devout and Learn'd
Who rose before us, and as Prophets burn'd,
Are all but Stories, which, awoke from Sleep
They told their comrades, and to Sleep return'd.

LXVII. Heav'n but the Vision of fulfill'd Desire,
And Hell the Shadow from a Soul on fire,
    Cast on the Darkness into which Ourselves,
So late emerged from, shall so soon expire.

XX. (The Second Edition)

The Palace that to Heav'n his pillars threw,
And Kings the forehead on his threshold drew—
I saw the solitary Ringdove there,
And "Coo, coo, coo," she cried; and "Coo, coo, coo."

XLIV. (The Second Edition)

Do you, within your little hour of Grace,
The waving Cypress in your Arms enlace.
  Before the Mother back into her arms
Fold, and dissolve you in a last embrace.

罗伯特·斯图尔特·谢里夫斯

Robert Stewart Sherriffs
（1906—1960）

英国漫画艺术家，擅长名人肖像画，以简单笔触还原人物神情，曾长期为英国著名漫画杂志《笨拙》绘制电影漫画。1947 年出版的《鲁拜集》由他绘制插图，评论界认为该作品代表了他绘画艺术的巅峰。

目录

译序

新版序

黄克孙

《鲁拜集》的原作者，波斯的奥玛珈音，生长于公元1048—1131年。这时代相当于中国的北宋，是伊斯兰文化的全盛时期。当年从欧洲入侵的十字军，在伊斯兰土地上，一般都遇到比自己先进的文明。

珈音是当时有名的数学家、天文学家；曾改造历法，提出太阳中心论，比哥白尼的理论早了三个多世纪。他写了一本《代数》，讨论二项式定理，并用几何方法来解三次方程$x^3 + 200x = 20x^2 + 2000$。“设x为未知”的想法盖源于此。

珈音也是诗人，可说是集沈括与苏东坡于一身。他写了一千多首“鲁拜”，就是波斯的四行诗。英国人费氏结楼（Edward FitzGerald, 1809—1883）选译了一百零一首。英译的《鲁拜集》不下十多种，但只有费氏译本广为传诵，因为它本身是好诗。

《鲁拜集》所表达的感情，包含了哲人的迷惑和诗人的潇洒。但文学，特别是诗，最终是对语言负责的。珈音的原作一定是波斯文学传统的产物。而费氏的译诗，空灵洒脱，怀古感慨，声调铿锵，韵脚美妙，则是英国文学登峰的作品。六十年前，少年时，我很向往费氏的诗。它构出的境界，往往在心中涌现。它的诗情，通过中文传统，很自然地就化为七言绝句。

二〇〇九年三月二十八日
美国麻省理工学院

第二版序

黄克孙

《鲁拜集》原作者奥玛珈音（1048—1131）生在十一世纪的波斯（即伊朗），相当于我国北宋时代。“鲁拜”指波斯的四行诗体。“珈音”是帐幕匠的意思。奥玛珈音的先人可能以造帐幕为业，但他本人是当时著名的天文学家和数学家。他留下的著作中，除了750首鲁拜外，还有《代数》、《欧基里德几何难题》、《论印度平立方根求法》、《金银比重》和《天文表》等书。在《代数》书中，他研究了三次和四次方程式的解法。

二十五岁时（公元1073年），他被波斯国王任命为天官。波斯于公元1079年颁布的历法是由他领导考订的。这历法比现在世界公用的阳历准确百分之三十。

无疑地，奥玛珈音主要的兴趣是天文和数学。鲁拜的写作，不过是旁及的活动而已。然而，现在人们知道他的名字，完全是为了他的鲁拜，特别是费氏结楼（Edward FitzGerald, 1809—1883）选译成英文的《鲁拜集》。奥玛珈音的鲁拜在当时波斯文坛上的地位我们不得而知，但费氏的译本，则是英国文学史上重要的著作。

费氏1826年毕业于英国剑桥大学，是诗人丁尼生（Tennyson）和小说家萨克雷（Thackeray）的同学。他对波斯文学，特别是对奥玛珈音鲁拜的兴趣，是由友人波斯学者爱德华·考埃尔（Edward Cowell）启发的。考埃尔自己也曾翻译过奥玛珈音的鲁拜十余首。他说："奥玛珈音的诗在世界文学史上占着独一的地位。难得的是一个大数学家纵情于诗章以为自娱。奥玛珈音包含了纯科学需要的最严密的思维和诗人所需的想象力和性灵。像罗马门神雅努斯（Janus）一样，他可以说是一个两面人。而这两面不但没有共同点，而且是互相矛盾的。"关于考埃尔的见解，以下再回来讨论。

费氏先在牛津大学图书馆得见奥玛珈音158首鲁拜原文，是1460年的手抄本。在1859年他选译了79首，刊行为《鲁拜集》。这集子当时并没有引起多大的兴趣，头版250本只卖了50本。剩下的200本被书店抛在旧书摊上以每本一分钱出售。适巧名诗人斯温伯恩（Swinburne）买了一本，读下大为欢赏，持示友人小说家乔治·梅瑞狄斯（George Meredith）。由于这两位文坛巨擘的表扬，费氏的译本从此闻名。其后，费氏在1868及1889年把《鲁拜集》添修重版二次。这里的中文翻译乃以最后一版为本。

当然，费氏并不是最早翻译奥玛珈音的人。早于十七世纪便有拉丁文的翻译。在十八世纪又有好几种德文和英文的译本。并且，费氏的翻译并不是最忠实于原文的。他自己也承认，往往把原文加以“润色”。例如，斯温伯恩最欣赏的第81首引用了伊甸天园的蛇的典故。这是原文没有的。但是，费氏的译文吸引了、迷住了世代的读者。原因很简单：费氏写的是诗，是在英国传统文学标准上站得住的好诗，他借奥玛珈音的灵感精神而重新创作。结果是词藻优美、可以传诵的诗章。相比之下，其他许多比较“忠实”的译本不是引人入胜的文学，而是古板的学者的文据。

奥玛珈音的灵感与精神在于什么？这问题对不同的人往往引出不同的反应。考埃尔的看法以上已提过，与费氏同时的评论家提到他“淡漠的悲哀”。有人说他是“泛神论者”，是“传统宗教束缚叛抗者”。这些意见大都反映评论者的背景，与奥玛珈音原意不一定有关系。正如卢梭赞赏的“崇高的野蛮人”，经过理想化的对象往往与原物的真相没有关系。同样地，我在这里只能表示个人对奥玛珈音的反应。

从中国传统的文哲学立场来看，奥玛珈音的许多形象都是“似曾相识”的。第一，四行诗体，马上使我联想到七言绝句。费氏韵律优美的译文更加强了这个联系。在内容上，我并没有体会到什么“泛神论”，什么“宗教的束缚”。这些欧洲的包袱是中国文化里没有的，波斯文化内也不一定有。奥玛珈音的诗意，使我想到孔子说的“逝者如斯夫，不舍昼夜”，也使我想起庄子说的“吾生也有涯，而知也无涯。以有涯逐无涯，殆已！”从而联想到李白的“夫天地者，万物之逆旅，光阴者，百代之过客，而浮生若梦，为欢几何”。所谓“淡漠的悲哀”，到底是有的。

但是，这些形象不过是“似曾相识”。《鲁拜集》有另一方面对于我是新鲜的。这熟识与新颖的汇合就是《鲁拜集》吸引力的来源。我意识到新颖的方面，在中国传统文学里没有的一方面，是一个数理学者的观点、信仰和感情。

精通天文和数学的奥玛珈音一定意识到，宇宙的规律是可以探知，并可以用严密而美妙的数学方式表示出来的。研究自然科学的人，都靠着一个不可少的信仰来鼓动及支持探索需要的苦功，就是，宇宙的真理是简单而美妙的；更根本一层的规律，更显得简单而美妙。这个信仰有宗教的力量，因而有感情的成分。

从另一方面说，研究科学者也是人，也经历体味到人事的复杂、命运的渺茫和人生的脆弱。他最高的逻辑告诉他，不管他剥去了多少层宇宙的秘密，不管他能多精密地计算天体的运动、物体的性质，他永远不能了解自己，永远不能了解人生最关键的问题：人生的目的是什么？生死究竟是怎样的一回事？这些问题需要能满足心灵的答案，主观的答案。这是客观科学不可能供给的。

一般人当然同样地有这些疑问，也同样地找不到答案。所不同的是，科学者知道数学在科学范围内的伟力。他有过求答成功的经验，因而树起一个比一般人较高的绳衡答案的标准。他深信宇宙是庄严、美妙、有一定法则的，但是人的死生问题是一扇永远打不开的门。这就是奥玛珈音的一贯的观点。

考埃尔所指出的奥玛珈音的独到处是正确的，就是，他的诗包含了科学者的观点与诗人的灵感。但是他所说的矛盾是错误的。科学最高的灵感与文学艺术最高的灵感是同源而一致的。它们的分别，在于表现的方式和技巧。

《鲁拜集》的翻译，我的出发点是作诗第一。人必先有感然后为诗。初读费氏的译诗时，我刚进研究院攻读理论物理学，阅读之下，心中怦然有感，如上所述。这快是四十年前的事情了。现承书林出版公司重刊旧译，因追个人感想一二，是为序。

一九八六年八月六日

美国麻省理工学院

题诗

草绿花红夏又深，满天星斗读珈音。
赤蛇头对苍龙尾，指点微茫天地心。
结楼居士最多情，重谱波斯古笛声。
伊览一城花似雪，家家传诵可兰经。
留得诗心伴玉壶，珈音仙去酒星孤。
一千年又匆匆过，生死玄机解也无。

——壬辰夏九月　克孙 题于康桥

暮雨长安古恨深，秋风如醉对清音。
狮旗夜展空沙晚，十丈离怀涨海心。
夜分风雨正关情，竟夕寒霜叶有声。
遥想明驼归路白，穹庐香暗对金经。
皓月沉天酒满壶，平沙万里一城孤。
帝前天使归何处，曾过长鲸大海无。

——一九五三年十二月十二日 劳干和韵

我爱黄君寄托深，能翻旧调出新音。
诗肠九转通今古，四海东西一样心。
抱瓮持花甚有情，醉来时发浩歌声。
夕阳大漠无边际，埋没明王剑与经。
醉乡门券酒三壶，饮者留名觚不孤。
我去君来犹故我，陶然相继岂空无。

——一九五四年十二月七日 杨联陞和韵

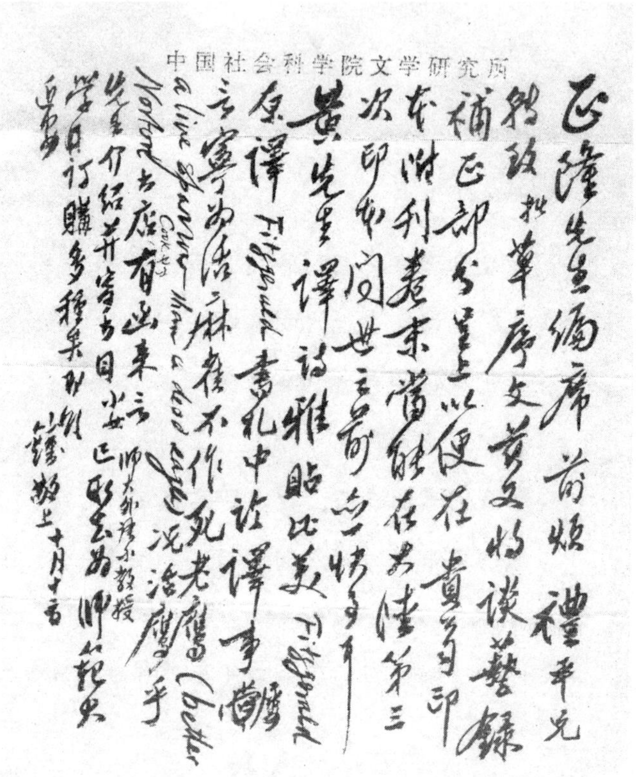

黄先生译诗雅贴比美FitzGerald原译。FitzGerald书札中论译事屡云“宁为活麻雀，不作死老鹰”（better a live sparrow than a dead eagle），况活鹰乎？

——钱锺书

鲁拜集

The Rubaiyat

Omar Khayyam

[波斯] 奥玛珈音 ———— 著

[英国] 爱德华·菲茨杰拉德 ———— 英译

[美国] 黄克孙 ———— 汉译

I

WAKE! For the Sun, who scatter'd into flight
The Stars before him from the Field of Night,
  Drives Night along with them from Heav'n, and strikes
The Sultan's Turret with a Shaft of Light.

一

醒醒游仙梦里人，

残星几点已西沉。

羲和骏马鬃如火，

红到苏丹塔上云[1]。

① 羲和：日御；日乘车，驾以六龙，羲和御之。苏丹：即Sultán，称为君主。（——编注：注释作者为苏正隆。）

II

Before the phantom of False morning died,
Methought a Voice within the Tavern cried,
    "When all the Temple is prepared within,
Why nods the drowsy Worshipper outside?"

二

一抹朝暾染四垂，

隔门客舍语依稀：

“生涯莫于金尊懒，

人易凋零酒易晞。”

III

And, as the Cock crew, those who stood before
The Tavern shouted—"Open then the Door!
    You know how little while we have to stay,
And, once departed, may return no more."

三

晨鸡一唱起南柯，
门外羁人击节歌：
“大地苍天原逆旅，
匆匆客岁已无多。”

IV

Now the New Year reviving old Desires,

The thoughtful Soul to Solitude retires,

  Where the WHITE HAND OF MOSES on the Bough

Puts out, and Jesus from the Ground suspires.

四

东风吹醒梦中人，
碧野平芜物又新。
摩世手伸千树白，
耶稣气吐一山春[1]。

① 摩世（Moses，又译摩西）：据传摩西手白如雪，故借喻白花。耶稣（Jesus）：据传说，耶稣气息，能抚愈创伤。

V

Iram indeed is gone with all it's Rose,
And Jamshyd's Sev'n-ring'd Cup where no one knows;
    But still a Ruby kindles in the Vine,
And many a Garden by the Water blows.

五

沉沉消息七环杯[1]，

伊览芳华尽势灰[2]。

唯有野花红似昔，

年年争向水边开。

① 七环杯：古波斯王Jamshyd有七环杯，以象七天、七星、七海。杯中常盛不死药。
② 伊览（Iram）：古波斯名城，现已埋没土下。

VI

And David's Lips are lockt; but in divine
High-piping Pehlevi, with "Wine! Wine! Wine!
    "Red Wine!"—the Nightingale cries to the Rose
That sallow check of hers to' incarnadine.

六

绕梁音绝歌人渺[1]，

犹有啼鹃格调高。

酒酒连声玫瑰酒，

欲将双颊染樱桃。

① 歌人：指古波斯名歌者David。

VII

Come, fill the Cup, and in the Fire of Spring
Your Winter-garmet of Repentance fling:
  The Bird of Time has but a little way
To flutter—and the Bird is on the Wing.

七

春火珠红酒里天，

心中块垒碎尊前。

白驹此去无多路，

岁月无情已着鞭。

VIII

Whether at Naishápúr or Babylon,
Whether the Cup with sweet of bitter run,
    The Wine of Life keeps oozing drop by drop,
The Leaves of Life keep falling one by one.

八

不问清瓢与浊瓢，

不分寒食与花朝[①]。

酒泉岁月涓涓尽，

枫树生涯叶叶飘。

① 寒食：清明前二日，俗禁火二日。花朝：俗以农历二月十二或二月十五为百花生日，称作花朝。

IX

Each Morn a thousand Roses brings, you say;
Yes, but where leaves the Rose of Yesterday?
    And this first Summer month that brings the Rose
Shall take Jamshyd and Kaikobád away.

九

闻道新红又吐葩，

昨宵玫瑰落谁家。

潇潇风信潇潇雨，

带得花来又葬花。

X

Well, let it take them! What have we to do
with Kaikobád the Great, or Kaikhosrú?
　Let Zál and Rustum bluster as they will,
Or Hátim call to Supper—heed not you.

十

汨罗江水伤心碧，

铜雀台花寂寞红[1]。

醉眼只宜看白日，

干卿底事哭英雄。

① 汨罗江：屈原自沉之处。铜雀台：魏武帝曹操所筑。魏武帝临终，遗命葬于西陵，与铜雀台相望，嘱诸子每月初一、十五登台望其墓。

XI

With me along the strip of Herbage strown
That just divides the desert from the sown,
    Where name of Slave and Sultan is forgot—
And Peace to Mahmúd on his golden Throne!

十一

平芜携手看黄沙，

牧草青青瀚海涯。

白屋朱袍浑不认[1]，

羲皇榻上是吾家。

① 白屋朱袍：平民与帝王。

XII

A Book of Verses underneath the Bough,
A Jug of Wine, a Loaf of Bread—and Thou
    Beside me singing in the Wilderness—
Oh, Wilderness were Paradise enow!

十二

一箪疏食一壶浆，

一卷诗书树下凉。

卿为阿侬歌瀚海，

茫茫瀚海即天堂。

XIII

Some for the Glories of This World; and some
Sigh for the Prophet's Paradise to come;
  Ah, take the Cash, and let the Credit go,
Nor heed the rumble of a distant Drum!

十三

三生事业尽朦胧，

一世浮华总落空。

今日有钱须买醉，

鼓声山外任隆隆[1]。

---

① 三生：前世、今世、来世。鼓声：喻遥远渺茫事。

XIV

Look to the blowing Rose about us— "Lo,
Laughing," she says, "into the world I blow,
At once the silken tassel of my Purse
Tear, and its Treasure on the Garden throw."

十四

玫瑰周遭向我开，
嫣然浅笑更低徊：
“看侬一解柔丝蕾，
红向千园万圃来。”

XV

And those who husbanded the Golden Grain,
And those who flung it to the Winds like rain,
  Alike to no such aureate Earth are turn'd
As, buried once, Men want dug up again.

十五

一杯浊酒无余恨，

死去谁怜金玉榇。

但见明珠出土来，

凄凉白骨无人问。

XVI

The Worldly Hope men set their Hearts upon
Turns Ashes—or it prospers; and anon,
  Like Snow upon the Desert's dusty Face
Lighting a little Hour or two—is gone.

十六

富贵当年想石崇[1]，

银鞍金络气如虹。

可怜雪落平沙里，

曾几何时日又中。

---

① 石崇：晋人，其富足可敌国。

XVII

Think, in this batter'd Caravanserai
Whose Portals are alternate Night and Day,
  How Sultan after Sultan with his Pomp
Abode his destined Hour, and went his way.

十七

乾坤寥落一穹庐，

日夜循环起太初。

多少英雄来复去，

锦衣华盖尽同途。

XVIII

They say the Lion and the Lizard keep
The courts where Jamshyd gloried and drank deep;
And Bahram, that great hunter—the Wild Ass
Stamps o'er his Head, but cannot break his Sleep.

十八

华表丹墀一例空[①]，

荒凉台榭走蛇虫。

虎踪今遍英雄墓，

无复惊闻李广弓。

① 华表：城郭、衙门、墓前等所立之柱识。丹墀：以丹漆阶上地曰丹墀。墀，音迟。

XIX

I sometimes think that never blows so red
The Rose as where some buried Cæsar bled;
    That every Hyacinth the Garden wears
Dropt in her Lap from some once lovely Head.

十九

红花底事红如此，

想是苌弘血里开[①]。

一地落英愁欲语：

“当年曾伴美人来。”

---

① 苌弘：周大夫，被杀后流血成石（或曰成碧），不见其尸。

XX

And this reviving Herb whose tender Green
Fledges the River-Lip on which we lean—
Ah, lean upon it lightly! for who knows
From what once lovely Lip it springs unseen!

二十

芳茵绿遍清江外，

弱草娇柔人欲采。

寄语行人莫损伤，

离离草下知谁在。

XXI

Ah, my Belovéd, fill the Cup that clears
TO-DAY of past Regrets and future Fears—
To-morrow? —Why, To-morrow I may be
Myself with Yesterday's Sev'n Thousand Years.

二十一

为卿斟酒洗尘缘，

莫问明朝事渺然。

我便明朝归去也，

相随昨日七千年。

XXII

For some we loved, the loveliest and the best
That from his Vintage rolling Time hath prest,
    Have drunk their Cup a Round or two before,
And one by one crept silently to Rest.

二十二

旧日湖山同醉客，
只今寥落已无多。
几杯饮罢魂销尽，
一一生涯酒里过。

XXIII

And we, that now make merry in the Room
They left, and Summer dresses in new bloom,
    Ourselves must we beneath the Couch of Earth
Descend, ourselves to make a Couch—for whom?

二十三

醉眠陵上草芊芊，
草下长埋古圣贤。
借问他年陵上客，
阿谁枕我骨头眠。

XXIV

Ah, make the most of what we yet may spend,
Before we too into the Dust descend;
    Dust into Dust, and under Dust, to lie,
Sans Wine, sans Song, sans Winger, and—sans End!

二十四

时恐秋霜零草莽，

韶华一旦随花葬。

微尘身世化微尘，

无酒无歌无梦想。

XXV

Alike for those who for TO-DAY prepare,
And those that after some TO-MORROW stare,
    A Muezzin from the Tower of Darkness cries
"Fools! Your Reward is neither Here nor There!"

二十五

饭颗山头饭颗生，

莲花灯下莲花起[①]。

忽闻棒喝一声来：

“道不在斯不在彼。”

① 饭颗山头饭颗生：喻为现世操劳。李白：“饭颗山头逢杜甫，头戴笠子日卓午。借问别来太瘦生，总为从前作诗苦。”莲花灯下莲花起：喻凝注来世，寄望往生莲花也。

XXVI

Why, all the Saint and Sages who discuss'd
Of the Two Worlds so wisely—they are thrust
    Like foolish Prophets forth; their words to Scorn
Are scatter'd, and their Mouths are stopt with Dust.

二十六

地狱天堂说未真，

恒恒贤哲几多人。

玲珑妙口今安在，

三尺泥中不复闻。

XXVII

Myself when young did eagerly frequent
Doctor and Saint, and heard great argument
    About it and about: but evermore
Came out by the same door where in I went.

二十七

少年执麈好谈玄，

邹子雕龙衍子天。

犹是野狐心未悟，

金函不学学逃禅[①]。

---

① 执麈：麈，音主，大鹿也，古人以麈尾作拂尘，清谈时手执麈尾，用以指授听众。邹子雕龙衍子天：齐人驺衍、驺奭善谈，人颂衍曰谈天衍，颂奭为雕龙奭。野狐：禅家谓以外道讲禅为野狐参禅。金函：《开元天宝遗事》："明皇忧勤国政……或有章疏……则探其理道优长者贮之金函中……时取读之。"逃禅：杜甫："苏晋长斋绣佛前，醉中往往爱逃禅。"

XXVIII

With them the Seed of Wisdom did I sow,
And with mine own hand wrought to make it grow;
   And this was all the Harvest that I reap'd—
"I came like Water, and like Wind I go."

二十八

辜负高人细解蒙，

希夷妙道未能通[1]。

此心本似无根草，

来是行云去是风。

---

① 希夷：听之不闻曰希，视之不见曰夷。

XXIX

Into this Universe, and *Why* not knowing,
Nor *Whence*, like Water willy-nilly flowing:
　And out of it, as Wind along the Waste,
I know not *Whither*, willy-nilly blowing.

二十九

浑噩生来非自宰，

生来天地又何之。

苍茫野水流无意，

流到何方水不知。

XXX

What, without asking, hither hurried *Whence*?
And, without asking, *Whither* hurried hence!
Oh, many a Cup of this forbidden Wine
Must drown the memory of that insolence!

三十

生本无因死亦空，

前身后世影朦胧。

何如十斛兰陵酒，

世界微尘一醉中[1]。

---

① 兰陵酒：兰陵产美酒。世界微尘：世界即宇宙，时间与空间的总称；微尘，极细之物。《楞严经》:“一切因果，世界微尘，因心成体。”

XXXI

Up from Earth's Centre through the Seventh Gate
I rose, and on the Throne of Saturn sate,
    And many a Knot unravel'd by the Road;
But not the Master-knot of Human Fate.

三十一

骑鹤神游阿母台，

七重天阙拂云来。

玉皇仙籍偷观尽，

司命天书揭不开。

XXXII

There was the Door to which I found no Key;
There was the Veil through which I might not see:
  Some little talk awhile of ME and THEE
There was—and then no more of THEE and ME.

三十二

太极庄严门矗立，

谷神缥缈帐深垂[1]。

微闻玉锁初开日，

度得红尘一客归。

① 谷神：谷中空虚之处，喻妙道。

XXXIII

Earth could not answer; nor the Seas that mourn
In flowing Purple, of their Lord forlorn;
    Nor rolling Heaven, with all his Signs reveal'd
And hidden by the sleeve of Night and Morn.

三十三

遍访乾坤总惘然，
天垂日月寂无言。
海涛悲涌深蓝色，
不答凡夫问太玄。

XXXIV

Then of the THEE IN ME who works behind
The Veil, I lifted up my hands to find
    A Lamp amid the Darkness; and I heard,
As from Without—"THE ME WITHIN THEE BLIND!"

三十四

闻道天人原合一，

微机分寸自能参。

如何缘业凭天结，

天道恢恢不可探。

XXXV

Then to the Lip of this poor earthen Urn
I lean'd, the Secret of my Life to learn:
    And Lip to Lip it Murmur'd—"While you live,
"Drink!—for once dead you never shall return."

三十五

红泥酒爵在唇边，
欲问前缘与后缘。
酒爵多情低语我：
“且将陶醉换华年。”

XXXVI

I think the Vessel, that with fugitive
Articulation answer'd, once did live,
    And drink; and Ah! The passive Lip I kiss'd
How many Kisses might it take—and give!

三十六

醉向冰壶问短长，

冰壶前世是刘郎[1]。

试看此日壶唇上，

多少脂痕渍粉香。

---

① 刘郎：刘伶，竹林七贤之一，放情肆志，性尤好酒。东汉刘晨与友入天台山，迷途，遇二女，设宴款待，行酒作乐。后求归，至家，子孙已七世矣。

XXXVII

For I remember stopping by the way
To watch a Potter thumping his wet Clay:
    And with its all-obliterated Tongue
It murmur'd— "Gently, Brother, gently, pray!"

三十七

南山采土冶为瓯，

土语啾啾说不休：

“我亦当年尘上客，

劳君雕琢要温柔。”

XXXVIII

And has not such a Story from of Old
Down Man's successive generations roll'd
    Of such a clod of saturated Earth
Cast by the Maker into Human mould?

三十八

不闻野老瓜棚下，

扪虱荒唐说鬼狐[①]。

见说天公能造化，

捏成骨肉自泥涂。

① 扪虱：从容不迫，无所畏忌。

XXXIX

And not a drop that from our Cups we throw
For Earth to drink of, but may steal below
    To quench the fire fo Anguish in some Eye
There hidden—far beneath, and long ago.

三十九

独对山川高酌罢，

临风细细酹余觞。

遥知几滴馨香酒，

必有泥中醉鬼尝。

XL

As then the Tulip for her morning sup
Of Heav'nly Vintage from the soil looks up,
    Do you devoutly do the like, till Heav'n
To Earth invert you—like an empty Cup.

四十

郁金花瓣朝天舞，
好趁晨风醉甘露。
日易盈昃露易晞[1]，
空垂残尊伤迟暮。

① 昃：日过午曰昃，日西也。晞：干。

XLI

Perplext no more with Human or Divine,
To-morrow's tangle to the winds resign,
    And lose your fingers in the tresses of
The Cypress-slender Minister of Wine.

四十一

成佛成仙渺果因，

明朝身世付烟云。

携壶浪迹山林上，

翠柏苍松供酒神。

XLII

And if the Wine you drink, the Lip you press,
End in what All begins and ends in—Yes;
    Think then you are TO-DAY what YESTERDAY
You were—TO-MORROW you shall not be less.

四十二

绿酒朱唇空过眼，

微尘原自化微尘。

今朝我即明朝我，

昨日身犹此日身。

XLIII

So when that Angel of the darker Drink
At last shall find you by the river-brink,
    And, offering his Cup, invite your Soul
Forth to your Lips to quaff—you shall not shrink.

四十三

茫茫天地有筵台，

司命高持黑酒杯。

酒过数巡应到我，

欣然尽饮莫徘徊。

XLIV

Why, if the Soul can fling the Dust aside,
And naked on the Air of Heaven ride,
    Were't not a Shame—were't not a Shame for him
In this clay carcase crippled to abide?

四十四

一朝蝉蜕余躯壳，

魂魄悠悠归碧落。

低首烟寰应自羞，

几年为此皮囊缚。

XLV

'Tis but a Tent where takes his one day's rest
A Sultan to the realm of Death addrest;
    The Sultan rises, and the dark Ferrash
Strikes, and prepares it for another Guest.

四十五

皮囊甲帐驻苏丹，

明日苏丹又西作[①]。

寥落穹庐野火中，

苏丹骏马飞沙漠。

① 西作：逝世。

XLVI

And fear not lest Existence closing your
Account, and mine, should know the like no more;
The Eternal Saki from that Bowl has pour'd
Millions of Bubbles like us, and will pour.

四十六

人来人去千秋事，

水泻危崖泡沫轻。

泡沫刹那俱幻灭，

华严瀑布永奔腾。

XLVII

When You and I behind the Veil are past,
Oh, but the long, long while the World shall last,
    Which of our Coming and Departure heeds
As the Sea's self should heed a pebble-cast.

四十七

一入重帏客渺然[①]，

无情天地自绵绵。

浮萍几点随波去，

不改苍茫海色玄。

① 重帏：据波斯传说，天堂有重帏，上帝高坐其后。

XLVIII

A Moment's Halt—a momentary taste
Of BEING from the Well amid the Waste—
And Lo!—the phantom Caravan has reach'd
The NOTHING it set out from—Oh, make haste!

四十八

平沙万里跸明驼，

寻得甘泉且放歌。

莫问远乡多少路，

远乡遥指是亡何。

XLIX

Would you that spangle of Existence spend
About THE SECRET—quick about it, Friend!
    A Hair perhaps divides the False and True—
And upon what, prithee, may life depend?

四十九

儒者登坛墨者逃，

由来真伪爽毫毛。

一生一死寻常事，

谁把天心示我曹。

L

A Hair perhaps divides the False and True;
Yes; and a single Alif were the Clue—
    Could you but find it—to the Treasure-house,
And peradventure to THE MASTER too;

五十

真伪由来爽一丝，

元真故故在希夷[1]。

凭君参尽人天理，

得见天心未可知。

① 故故：屡屡。

LI

Whose secret Presence through Creation's veins
Running, Quicksilver-like eludes your pains;
    Taking all shapes from Máh to Máhi; and
They change and perish all—but He remains;

五十一

月明海上化仙禽，

忽幻鱼龙入水深[1]。

世界刹那千万相，

盎然不变是天心。

① 月化鱼：波斯俗以“月化鱼”喻变迁。

LII

A moment guess'd—then back behind the Fold
Immerst of Darkness round the Drama roll'd
    Which, for the Pastime of Eternity,
He doth Himself contrive, enact, behold.

五十二

浩荡天门瞬息开，
千秋蝼蚁浪疑猜[1]。
云山几度成沧海，
造化红尘游戏来。

① 蝼蚁：喻微小。

LIII

But if in vain, down on the stubborn floor
Of Earth, and up to Heav'n's unopening Door,
    You gaze TO-DAY, while You are You—how then
TO-MORROW, when You shall be You no more?

五十三

举首叩天天不语，

低头问地地无闻。

即今俯仰犹迷惘，

何况他年墓里人。

LIV

Waste not your Hour, nor in the vain pursuit
Of This and That endeavour and dispute;
    Better be jocund with the fruitful Grape
Than sadden after none, or bitter, Fruit.

五十四

垦道求真终不获，

便成果实亦酸辛。

何如独到南山上，

摘取葡萄祭酒神。

LV

You know, my Friend, with what a brave Carouse
I made a Second Marriage in my house;
    Divorced old barren Reason from my Bed,
And took the Daughter of the Vine to Spouse.

五十五

落落心怀久不开，
酒酣拔剑断琴台。
忍教智慧成离妇，
新娶葡萄公主来。

LVI

For "Is" and "IS-NOT" though with Rule and Line
And "UP-AND-DOWN" by Logic I define,
    Of all that one should care to fathom, I
Was never deep in anything but—Wine.

五十六

是非原在有无中，

竭想穷思总是空。

借问一心何所好，

满杯春酒漾娇红。

LVII

Ah, but my Computations, People say,
Reduce the Year to better reckoning? —Nay,
'Twas only strking from the Calendar
Unborn To-morrow, and dead Yesterday.

五十七

曾司北斗与招摇，
玉历天衡略整调[1]。
纸上淋漓纵醉笔，
勾除昨日与明朝。

① 北斗与招摇：皆星名。玉历天衡：天文历法。

LVIII

And lately, by the Tavern Door agape,
Came shining through the Dusk an Angel Shape
  Bearing a Vessel on his Shoulder; and
He bid me taste of it; and 'twas—the Grape!

五十八

蓬门昨夜有人敲，

王母仙童馈绿醪。

翠色新瓷包锦袱，

启瓶一酌是葡萄。

LIX

The Grape that can with Logic absolute
The Two-and-Seventy jarring Sects confute:
    The sovereign Alchemist that in a trice
Life's leaden metal into Gold transmute;

五十九

葡萄美酒紫金钟，

药鼎丹炉笑葛洪[①]。

输与此时一杯酒，

琴心三叠十年功。

---

① 葛洪：晋人，好神仙术，赴交趾炼丹，丹成尸解。

LX

The mighty Mahmúd, Allah-breathing Lord,
That all the misbelieving and black Horde
    Of Fears and Sorrows that infest the Soul
Scatters before him with his whirlwind Sword.

六十

酒降人间感上苍，

一杯洗尽九回肠。

钟馗手秉旋风剑，

独立天庭百鬼惶。

LXI

Why, be this Juice the growth of God, who dare
Blaspheme the twisted tendril as a Snare?
  A Blessing, we should use it, should we not?
And if a Curse—why, then, who set it there?

六十一

上帝传符造甘酒，
杜康降自九天遥[1]。
若非天旨分明在，
谁敢皇皇犯戒条。

① 杜康：周人，善造酒。

LXII

I must abjure the Balm of Life, I must,
Scared by some After-reckoning ta'en on trust,
    Or lured with Hope of some Diviner Drink,
To fill the Cup—when crumbled into Dust!

六十二

天上何时禁酒觞，

人间甘露我偷尝。

拚将缥缈三生债，

换得千秋醉道场。

LXIII

Oh threats of Hell and Hopes of Paradise!
One thing at least is certain—*This* Life flies;
    One thing is certain and the rest is Lies;
The Flower that once has blown for ever dies.

六十三

碧落黄泉皆妄语，

三生因果尽荒唐。

浊醪以外无真理，

一谢花魂再不香。

LXIV

Strange, is it not? That of the myriads who
Before us pass'd the door of Darkness through,
　Not one returns to tell us of the Road,
Which to discover we must travel too.

六十四

道失冥关谁借问，

了无归客说岖崎。

漫漫别路深如许，

寂寞行人只自知。

LXV

The Revelations of Devout and Learn’d
Who rose before us, and as Prophets burn’d
Are all but Stories, which, awoke from Sleep
They told their comrades, and to Sleep return’d.

六十五

哲人攲枕漫游仙[1]，
睡眼惺忪说太玄。
地狱天堂言未已，
转身榻上又高眠。

---

① 攲：侧倚、斜靠。攲，音欺。

LXVI

I sent my Soul through the Invisible,
Some letter of that After-life to spell:
　And by and by my Soul return'd to me,
And answer'd "I Myself am Heav'n and Hell:"

六十六

欲寻身后路茫茫，
自遣离魂到大荒。
魂魄归来唯一语：
“我兼地狱与天堂。”

LXVII

Heav'n but the Vision of fulfill'd Desire,
And Hell the Shadow from a Soul on fire,
    Cast on the Darkness into which Ourselves,
So late emerged from, shall so soon expire.

六十七

醉抛衣带成河汉，

泪洒云山作汴湘。

火借愁心为地狱，

酒空尘欲即天堂。

LXVIII

We are no other than a moving row
Of Magic Shadow-shapes that come and go
    Round with the Sun-illumined Lantern held
In Midnight by the Master of the Show;

六十八

琉璃冰罩转玲珑，
巧镂山河大匠功。
中有光明灯一盏，
纸人泥马影憧憧[1]。

---

① 憧憧：往来不绝貌。憧，音冲。

LXIX

But helpless Pieces of the Game He plays
Upon this Chequer-board of Nights and Days;
    Hither and thither moves, and checks, and slays,
And one by one back in the Closet lays.

六十九

纵横日夜为棋局，
枰上千秋劫正浓。
转换腾那犹未了[①]，
残棋一一入壶中。

---

① 劫：棋弈中紧迫的关键。腾那：变易。

LXX

The Ball no question makes of Ayes and Noes,
But Here or There as strikes the Player goes;
    And He that toss'd you down into the Field,
He knows about it all—HE knows—HE knows!

七十

眼看乾坤一局棋，

满枰黑白子离离。

铿然一子成何劫，

惟有苍苍妙手知。

LXXI

The Moving Finger writes; and, having writ,
Moves on: nor all your Piety nor Wit
    Shall lure it back to cancel half a Line,
Nor all your Tears wash out a Word of it.

七十一

冥冥有手写天书，
彩笔无情挥不已。
流尽人间泪几千，
不能洗去半行字。

LXXII

And that inverted Bowl they call the sky,
Whereunder crawling coop'd we live and die,
    Lift not your hands to It for help—for It
As impotently moves as you or I.

七十二

浑圆天盖碧深沉，

月运星移古至今。

莫向苍天求解脱，

苍天旋转不由心。

LXXIII

With Earth's first Clay They did the Last Man knead,
And there of the Last Harvest sow'd the Seed:
    And the first Morning of Creation wrote
What the Last Dawn of Reckoning shall read.

七十三

天化劳人泥与水，

身渗苦水到穷途。

云山沧海何年尽，

都在鸿蒙纸上书。

LXXIV

YESTERDAY *This* Day's Madness did prepare;
TO-MORROW'S Silence, Triumph, or Despair:
    Drink! For you know not whence you came, nor why:
Drink! For you know not why you go, nor where.

七十四

风云一一安排好，

世界如荼入眼来[1]。

痛饮不闻狂客问，

明朝何处化尘埃。

---

① 如荼：盛大貌。

LXXV

I tell you this—When, started from the Goal,
Over the flaming shoulders of the Foal
    Of Heav'n Parwin and Mushtari they flung,
In my predestined Plot of Dust and Soul.

七十五

天马长嘶振鬣毛，

溟蒙驰道接云高。

神明马上伸天手，

摘取星辰向我抛[1]。

---

① 星辰：指珈音所属宫位。

LXXVI

The Vine had struck a fibre: which about
If clings my Being—let the Dervish flout;
    Of my Base metal may be filed a Key,
That shall unlock the Door he howls without.

七十六

神山一树众生出，
我是仙桃树上虫。
偷得人间金锁钥，
醉眠内府宝藏中。

LXXVII

And this I know: whether the one True Light
Kindle to Love, or Wrath—consume me quite,
    One Flash of It within the Tavern caught
Better than in the Temple lost outright.

七十七

心中幻灭有明灯，
幻出人间爱与憎。
灯影酒中犹照我，
神明坛上见何曾。

LXXVIII

What! out of senseless Nothing to provoke
A conscious Something to resent the yoke
    Of unpermitted Pleasure, under pain
Of Everlasting Penalties, if broke!

七十八

天公取土雕成我，

爱欲痴嗔泥里和。

争又人间设果因，

三生却问他生过。

LXXIX

What! from his helpless Creature be repaid
Pure Gold for what he lent him dross-allay'd—
    Sue for a Debt he never did contract,
And cannot answer—Oh the sorry trade!

七十九

天赐人间自在身，

形骸放浪是元真。

此生哪有他生债，

未向苍天借一文。

LXXX

Oh Thou, who didst with pitfall and with gin
Beset the Road I was to wander in,
    Thou wilt not with Predestined Evil round
Enmesh, and then impute my Fall to Sin!

八十

千山歧路何人辟，

要问冥冥造化来。

鞭底苍茫征路远，

乱蓬好自为吾开。

LXXXI

Oh, Thou, who Man of baser Earth didst make,
And ev'n with Paradise devise the Snake:
    For all the Sin wherewith the Face of Man
Is blaken'd, Man's Forgiveness give—and take!

八十一

苍穹含缺女娲嗟，

伊甸天园尚有蛇。

草草众生原帝力，

谁教为善与为邪。

LXXXII

As under cover of departing Day
Slunk hunger-stricken Ramazan away,
    Once more within the Potter's house alone
I stood surrounded by the Shapes of Clay.

八十二

晨昏一例醉中眠，
过尽凄凉九月天[1]。
又访村家陶匠去，
泥瓮秋客对萧然。

① 九月：伊斯兰历九月斋戒，名为Ramazán。

LXXXIII

Shapes of all Sorts and Sizes, great and small,
That stood along the flood and by the wall;
    And some loquacious Vessels were; and some
Listen'd perhaps, but never talk'd at all.

八十三

红猩绿翠采姿多，

短缶长瓶壁上罗。

黄目无言垂醉眼[1]，

泥壶开口唱山歌。

---

① 黄目：铜器之一种。

LXXXIV

Said one among them—"Surely not in vain
My substance of the common Earth was ta'en
   And to this Figure moulded, to be broke,
Or trampled back to shapeless Earth again."

八十四

“弯弯壶嘴似蛾眉，
手做泥壶为阿谁。
随手捏成随手碎，
到头还是一堆泥。”

LXXXV

Then said a Second—"Ne'er a peevish Boy
Would break the Bowl from which he drank in joy;
And He that with his hand the Vessel made
Will surely not in after Wrath destroy."

八十五

瓦尊壁上曼声呼:
“酒客犹知惜酒壶,
多少匠心成一器,
无端谁忍碎无辜。”

LXXXVI

After a momentary silence spake
Some Vessel of a more ungainly Make;
    "They sneer at me for leaning all awry;
What! Did the hand then of the Potter shake?"

八十六

古瓶鷈甈背穹隆[1]，

独坐尘埃诉苦衷：

“想是匠人年已老，

摩挲雕琢手龙钟。”

① 鷈甈：音孽悟，动摇不安貌。穹隆：穹然而隆起；长曲貌。

LXXXVII

Whereat some one of the loquacious Lot—
I think a Sufi pipkin—waxing hot—
　“All this of Pot and Potter—Tell me then,
Who is the Potter, pray and who the Pot?”

八十七

小壶颜色火烧云，

谈笑悬河水泻银：

“漫说陶人与陶器，

孰为陶器孰陶人。”

LXXXVIII

“Why,” said another, “Some there are who tell
Of one who threatens he will toss to Hell
    The luckless Pots he marr’d in making—Pish!
He’s a Good Fellow, and ’twill all be well.”

八十八

说法泥瓮貌岸然：

“成材成器总由天。

残壶废碗都抛去，

抛到无情火焰边。”

LXXXIX

"Well," murmured one, "Let whoso make or buy,
My Clay with long Oblivision is gone dry:
    But, fill me with the old familiar Juice,
Methinks I might recover by and by!"

八十九

寂寞凋零一断壶，

年年愁待酒家胡[1]：

“请君为我勤斟酒，

垂老心肠久已枯。”

---

① 酒家胡：酒家之姬也。

XC

So while the Vessels one by one were speaking
The little Moon look'd in that all were seeking:
    And then they jogg'd each other, "Brother! Brother!
Now for the Porter's shoulder-knot a-creaking!"

九十

月照千家户半开，

壶尊无语静尘埃。

鞋声细碎闻窗外，

疑是飘零酒客来。

XCI

Ah, with the Grape my fading Life provide,
And wash the Body whence the Life has died,
  And lay me, shrouded in the living Leaf,
By some not unfrequented Garden-side.

九十一

一旦魂归万事空，

劳君倾酒洗萍踪。

遗身愿裹葡萄叶，

葬在名花怒放中。

XCII

That ev'n my buried Ashes such a snare
Of Vintage shall fling up into the Air
    As not a True-believer passing by
But shall be overtaken unaware.

九十二

死化寒灰带酒香，

河山千古葬遗觞。

他年游子来凭吊，

犹得坟前醉一场。

XCIII

Indeed the Idols I have loved so long
Have done my credit in this World much wrong:
    Have drown'd my Glory in a shallow Cup,
And sold my Reputation for a Song.

九十三

不事神明事酒魔，
前尘后事任蹉跎。
借来年命偿杯酒，
卖去浮名买醉歌。

XCIV

Indeed, indeed, Repentance oft before
I swore—but was I sober when I swore?
    And then and then came Spring, and Rose-in-hand
My thread-bare Penitence apieces tore.

九十四

平生悔恨我何曾，

醉里模糊说不清。

见说人间春又到，

尊前莫作懊侬声。

XCV

And much as Wine has play'd the Infidel,
And robb'd me of my Robe of Honour—Well
  I wonder often what the Vintners buy
One half so precious as the stuff they sell.

九十五

酒误浮名犹爱酒，

转怜卖酒村前叟。

卖来不过几文钱，

何物能如酒一斗。

XCVI

Yet Ah, that Spring should vanish with the Rose!
That Youth's sweet-scented Manuscript should close!
    The Nightingale that in the branches sang,
Ah, whence, and whither flown again, who knows!

九十六

墓里古人浑不语，

杨花榭后飘香絮。

子规啼尽一春心，

飞到天涯何处去。

XCVII

Would but the Desert of the Fountain yield
One glimpse—if dimly, yet indeed, reveal'd,
  To which the fainting Traveller might spring,
As springs that trampled herbage of the field!

九十七

古野犹生春草绿，

茫茫大漠何寥哉。

行人远道凄凉甚，

可有清泉慰客来。

XCVIII

Would but some wingéd Angel ere too late
Arrest the yet unfolded Roll of Fate,
　And make the stern Recorder otherwise
Enregister, or quite obliterate!

九十八

愿见仙人启玉楼，

天书细细写从头。

生涯不为重斟酌，

便把微身一笔勾。

XCIX

Ah Love! could you and I with Him conspire
To grasp this sorry Scheme of Things entire,
    Would not we shatter it to bits—and then
Re-mould it nearer to the Heart's Desire!

九十九

梦游昨夜到天池，
欲借神明剑一枝。
斩碎三千愁世界，
从头收拾旧须弥。

C

Yon rising Moon that looks for us again—
How oft hereafter will she wax and wane;
    How oft hereafter rising look for us
Through this same Garden—and for *one* in vain!

一百

明月多情伴客身，

人来人去月无闻，

从今几度黄昏月，

遍照园林少一人。

CI

And when like her, oh Sáki, you shall pass
Among the Guests Star-scatter'd on the Grass,
  And in your joyous errand reach the spot
Where I made One—turn down an empty Glass!

一百零一

酒僮酒僮劝客来，
座中无我莫徘徊。
醉翁去后余何物，
一只空空覆酒杯。

译后记

黄克孙

上奥玛珈音《鲁拜集》一百又一首。根据费氏结楼（E. FitzGerald）第五英译本衍译，旁参费氏第一译本及其他散文英译本。

参考材料见

THE SUFISTIC QUATRAINS OF OMAR KHAYYAM, IN DEFINITIVE FORM,

Including the translations of

Edward FitzGerald (101 quatrains) with Edward Heron-Allen's analysis

E.H.Whinefield (500 quatrains)

J.B. Nicolas (464 quatrains)

(M. Walter Dunne, Publisher, New York and London, 1903)

ISBN 978-7-5447-8375-0

9 787544 783750 01>

凤凰出版传媒网:www.ppm.cn

定价:65.00元